The
LAST
HAWK

ELIZABETH WEIN

For Jared (The Great Houweini)

First published in 2021 in Great Britain by
Barrington Stoke Ltd
18 Walker Street, Edinburgh, EH3 7LP

www.barringtonstoke.co.uk

Text © 2021 Elizabeth Gatland

A CIP catalogue record for this book is available from the British Library upon request

ISBN: 978-1-78112-955-5

Printed by Hussar Books, Poland

CONTENTS

PROLOGUE

Ingrid Hartman's Notes for a Confession – France, July 1944

It's strange to be a prisoner and yet to have stopped being afraid. I suppose that should tell me I've made the right decision.

But I don't know what my future holds – it's a blank sheet ahead of me. I can't be sure of anything. I have no idea what will happen to me – where I'll end up and if I'll be allowed to fly again. I don't think I can ever go home – and by home, I don't mean to my family. I don't mean to the village where I was born and grew up. I mean I'll never be able to go back to Germany, whether we win or lose the war.

Perhaps my own decision will change what happens. I hope it *does*. But whatever happens, I won't be welcome in Germany any more.

I might be a prisoner, but my name is still Ingrid Hartman, and I am still seventeen years old. I still have straight brown hair cut short so it fits easily under a flying helmet, a pale face with a pointed nose and bright brown eyes that gave me the nickname "Flying Mouse".

But who am I now? I'm no longer the stuttering girl in the corner of the schoolroom, the one who's always looking at the sky. I'm not the dreamer who's happier with birds than people, who watches hawks for hours and lets sparrows eat crumbs from the palms of her hands. I'm no longer the student at the gliding school with her head in the clouds. I'm a refugee now – an enemy prisoner of war. Would my own father call me a traitor?

I'd like to believe he would not, if he knew the truth. I'd rather think of myself as a patriot – fighting for my country against the monsters who pushed it into the fearful corner it stands in now.

I told the interrogators from the US Army that I would write down my story for them.

That's what I'm going to do.

PART 1: *The Fledgling*

CHAPTER 1

My journey began last winter, in February of 1944, in our pretty Alpine village of Ulmenhain. My mother died six months before. My journey began because the telephone and the doorbell rang at almost exactly the same time.

My father was out at a meeting with the Ulmenhain mayor, and I was alone in the house with Minna, our housekeeper. It was snowing hard. When the telephone rang, I didn't pay any attention. I was forbidden to answer it because of my stutter. I was in the living room, engrossed in a book I'd borrowed from my friend Emil. He'd given it to me early last summer and I'd already read it five times, but it never grew dull – partly because I loved the book, and partly because I missed Emil and liked to imagine what he'd thought when he read it.

It was called *Wind, Sand and Stars* and was written by a French pilot named Antoine de Saint-Exupéry. I was in the middle of a dramatic true story about how Antoine's plane crashed in the desert and he nearly died of thirst. I hardly heard the telephone. A moment later, I hardly heard the doorbell. I assumed Minna would get the door as well as the phone. That was part of her job.

After a pause, the doorbell rang again.

I looked up from my book this time, realising that Minna must still be on the telephone, upstairs in my father's study. I wasn't supposed to answer the door, because I found it so difficult to talk to people. But there was no one else in the house.

As I hesitated, I heard the door open and snow being stamped from someone's boots. There was the sound of angry footsteps crossing the wooden floor of the hall.

I stood up and put down my book. Who had let himself in? Who would do that apart from my father?

A tall man suddenly marched into the front room where I was sitting. He was older than my father, with thin blond hair combed over his shining scalp. He wore polished black boots and a long brown overcoat and red armband – he was a Nazi Party official. His peaked cap was in his hand, and he shook snow from it over my mother's wool carpet. His entire head was red, even the skin that showed beneath his thin hair.

"Are you deaf, girl?" the man barked at me. "I have rung the doorbell twice and knocked as well, and you have been in here the whole time ignoring me! Are you Arno Hartman's daughter? What shameful disrespect!"

I was horrified, realising that he must have seen me in the window. A Nazi Party official had banged at our front door, and he thought I'd ignored him on purpose! It would get my father in trouble as well as me.

"I beg your p-p-pardon!" I burst out. "I thought our housekeeper would c-c-come—"

"Is that how a polite young German girl greets an important elder?" growled the angry man.

I nearly choked as I realised I'd forgotten to say "*Heil Hitler*". It should have been the first thing I said. That's how you were supposed to greet everybody, not just Nazi Party officials. You could get reported to the police if you didn't say it.

Instead of trying to apologise again, I gave the Nazi salute and gasped out, "*Heil Hitler!*"

At that moment Minna came bustling downstairs and into the room.

"Region Leader Wulfsen!" Minna said. She knew exactly who the officer was and why he was there. "I've just had a telephone call from Herr Hartman." So it had been my father himself on the phone – what irony! "He's on his way back from the mayor's office now and apologises for his late arrival. Please, let us make you comfortable while you wait."

Minna turned to me. Her face was pale, but her expression was neutral. "Ingrid, would you make coffee for our guest?" Minna said. "I'll show Region Leader Wulfsen upstairs to your father's study. Please get a tray ready in the kitchen, and I'll come back down to fetch it."

I bowed to Region Leader Wulfsen before I left the room, and gave Minna a tight but grateful smile as I slipped past her to get to the kitchen. She'd saved me from having a conversation with a Nazi official – something my father and mother had spent the last ten years trying to avoid.

CHAPTER 2

Having a conversation probably seems like a small thing – how much could it matter whether anyone outside our household noticed how I stuttered?

But keeping my mouth shut so no one would notice me was actually a matter of life and death.

I have stuttered since I began to talk. At first my parents did not worry about it – my father told me that he'd had the same problem, but by the time he went to secondary school, his stutter had vanished. Sadly I didn't grow out of my speaking difficulties so easily.

I was six years old when Hitler and the Nazi Party came to power in Germany. Many of the laws in our country changed, and many new ones were introduced. A lot of them were aimed at keeping the people of Germany pure and healthy. Hitler wanted to ensure our nation was free from physical or mental disabilities.

My mother was a nurse who worked in the Ulmenhain Youth Hospital. It was a special home for children who were not able to learn things quickly. One of the new Nazi laws meant that these children all had to have an operation called sterilisation. Then they would never be able to have children of their own and therefore not pass on their learning difficulties to a new generation.

I don't remember when my parents began to worry that this law might apply to me. But I do remember my mother coming home in the evenings after her day at the hospital, sitting over her sewing and crying. I thought it was because the children at the hospital were forced to have these unfair and painful operations. Later, I knew that she was also crying because she was worried about me.

In 1939, when I was twelve, Hitler and the Nazi Party led Germany into war, and things at the hospital got worse. At first, my mother and the other carers were told to stop doing some of their tasks, such as giving the children regular baths and clean sheets and clean clothes. Children who were ill were not given medicine. All the children were given poor food, and less and less of it.

It was not long before some of the children died.

The Ulmenhain Youth Hospital was shut down about a year after the war started. The grand building was now to be used as a place for wounded German soldiers to recover. All the children who still lived at the hospital were taken away in buses. Other people from our village were taken with them. There was the butcher's young sister, whose legs were so weak that she went about on crutches. The street cleaner with no parents who wouldn't ever stop sweeping unless someone told him he was finished. Even the mayor's second son, who was blind and deaf.

The police *said* they were all going to be sent someplace where they'd be taken care of. But then the mayor and the butcher both got death notices at the same time, telling them their loved ones had died of pneumonia. Nobody ever heard anything more about the harmless street sweeper or the vanished children from the hospital.

My stutter had always made me shy, and my mousey looks didn't help. But as I grew older, the stutter began to make me scared as well as shy. I learned to keep quiet. I did my schoolwork as carefully as I could so I wouldn't be told off and made to speak in class. It wouldn't matter that my father was the district administrator for education if some important Nazi decided I was disabled – the mayor hadn't been able to save his son.

My mother was determined to prove that I was a solid and useful German citizen. She had a cousin who was the head instructor at the small Ulmenhain Gliding School, which perched on a mountain meadow above our village.

Maybe my parents wouldn't have let their daughter take flying lessons if they hadn't felt such a strong need for me to prove myself. But they did, and I loved gliding. I was good at it. Mother's cousin, Jonni, was a patient instructor, and he always looked out for me. There was no secondary school in our village, so from the age of fourteen I spent much of my time at the gliding school. I kept the floor clean when mud and slush got tracked in, and I was always ready with a hot drink for the students when they came in to get warm after a long flight.

In exchange, I was allowed to fly in the flimsy school gliders. Cousin Jonni sometimes even let me fly in the sturdier Crane glider with the schoolboys who would one day become air force pilots. I'd guide them into the air as if I were an instructor myself.

I was confident in the air. But all that confidence and talent vanished when I had to speak with an angry Nazi official on the ground. A man who'd had to let himself into my own home because I was too scared to answer the door.

As Minna now took Region Leader Wulfsen upstairs, I focused on the task of making coffee for him. I was thankful that Minna had given me the chance to escape.

The "coffee" was ground from a mixture of roasted barley and acorns – it was more than two years since we'd had any real coffee in Ulmenhain. My mother had taught me how to make this pretend stuff just the way her mother had taught her to do it in the Great War nearly thirty years earlier.

I paced the kitchen nervously while the coffee heated. Across the courtyard I could see the empty stables. We no longer kept any horses. They'd been taken away to serve the army around the same time I'd killed the last of my mother's chickens to eat. We rarely had meat now, and no hens meant no eggs. There was little milk, despite living in a village in the countryside. Our main foods were homegrown turnips and potatoes and cabbages.

Last spring, my mother had helped plant the food that we were eating this winter – before she became so ill that she could no longer get out of bed. Knowing she'd planted it comforted me and made me feel miserable at the same time.

The birds were hungry too. The snow was coming down, but I could see that there was a pair of blue tits pecking at the crumbs I'd left for them on the bird table by the empty stable.

The sight of these small, winged creatures working hard to keep themselves alive lifted my spirits. I could fly too. When the snow stopped, I could climb the hill to the gliding school and borrow a plane and swoop over the white mountainsides, as carefree as a small bird.

I brewed the pretend coffee. I was setting the pot on a tray along with one of my mother's pretty flowered china cups when I heard the front door open again.

Thank goodness – my father was home.

I let out a sigh of relief and set another cup on the tray. Minna had said she was going to come down to get it, so I wouldn't have to face the Nazi officer's anger again.

But I knew I would soon have to face my father's anger.

CHAPTER 3

It was half an hour before Region Leader Wulfsen left the house. I waited until I'd heard him say his farewells and the heavy front door bang shut, and then I tiptoed into the hall to greet my father.

"Come up to my study, Ingrid," he said. "I need to speak to you." He turned and clattered up the stairs, and I had to follow him.

My father, Arno Hartman, was strict and careful. He was good at his job as district administrator for education. I loved him, and he was a kind man, but he was not warm. He was always stiff and formal even with people he cared about. Since my mother's death six months before, he hardly spoke and spent more and more time wrapped up in his work.

Now I stood before him in his dark, wood-panelled study. The snow had stopped falling and the clouds suddenly cleared, the winter afternoon now bright with sunlight. My father sat at his desk with his back to the broad window. The shutters were open to let in light and air, and the room was as cold as a cave.

"Do you know who that visitor was?" my father asked me in a low voice.

I shook my head. I knew Region Leader Wulfsen's name, but I didn't know what his job was or why he would be meeting with my father. Shaking my head was easier than explaining all this. I tried to make wordless answers whenever I could to avoid speaking.

"He was Hans Wulfsen," my father said, "the Region Leader for the Nazi Party Ministry of Propaganda. I have to report to him on how we're promoting the Nazi Party in our local schools."

I nodded to show that I understood.

"Do you know what Region Leader Wulfsen said to me?" my father asked.

Again I shook my head.

My father drew in his breath sharply before he spoke. "He said, '*Your daughter is a disgrace to Germany.*'"

My father didn't raise his voice, but I could sense his fear and anger from the tense way he leaned forward at his desk and by the deep, shaking breaths that he was taking.

"There wasn't much I could do to argue against it," my father continued. "You barely speak, Ingrid. You spend your life wasting crumbs on wild birds and chasing hawks you'll never catch. I told Region Leader Wulfsen you are strong and able, but all he has seen is that you sat daydreaming while he waited on our doorstep, that you forgot your '*Heil Hitler*' when he came in, and that you could not speak a sentence straight."

My father stopped for a moment to take a breath and I tried to answer him.

"B-b-but—"

My stuttering suddenly made my father furious.

"Be silent and let me finish, Ingrid!" he snapped at me.

I pressed my lips together.

"If that man believes you are mentally or genetically lacking, he could end your life, Ingrid," my father said. "He could do it without a moment's hesitation or guilt, with no more than a letter or a telephone call. You would be taken away in a bus like the mayor's son, and perhaps a month later I would be told that you had died of pneumonia. Who knows what really happened to those poor souls from the Ulmenhain Youth Hospital? Perhaps we wouldn't even wonder about it if we didn't know what had happened there before the war. The mayor *asked* for his son to be taken away! It is hard not to judge him, knowing what I know. I could do nothing to stop it if they were to come for you and force you out of this house. The Nazi Party's word is law, and now they have labelled you '*a disgrace to Germany*'. That in itself could get you sent to a camp as a political prisoner. It could be the end of you."

Everyone in Germany knew about the harsh work camps set up by the Nazis when Hitler came to power in 1933. The Gestapo secret police filled them with people who went against the government or didn't conform to Nazi standards.

I could hear the fear and frustration in my father's voice, and I understood. The thought of being marked as a troublemaker by anyone in the Nazi Party terrified me.

"I'll b-b-be eighteen this year," I said.

I took deep breaths, trying to calm my very real fear.

"Then I can be certified as a g-g-gliding instructor. What could be more p-p-patriotic than helping young air force p-p-pilots?"

"Can you do that now?" my father asked me seriously.

"Not until I'm eighteen," I said. "In six months."

"Ask Jonni Becker at the gliding school if he can certify you sooner," my father said. But then he sighed. He knew as well as I did that Cousin Jonni couldn't break official rules even to try to save my life. "Ask him if he can promise you a place there as an instructor. Perhaps Jonni can give you an official job at the clubhouse – 'junior instructor' or something like that."

I nodded. We didn't speak for a moment. I wondered if my father felt the same sense of terrified urgency that I did.

When my father spoke again, he didn't sound as if he was panicking. But he made it clear he didn't want me to waste any time.

"The sun is shining," my father said. "Don't wait until tomorrow. Go now."

CHAPTER 4

As the weather had cleared, I knew Cousin Jonni would probably be fitting in a few late flights before it got dark. I wanted to obey my father and talk to Cousin Jonni as soon as possible. So I went downstairs, unhooked my leather jacket and gloves from the coatrack and headed out to the gliding school.

The young men of our village had left or been taken away to become soldiers, and any boy over fifteen could go away to work as air force ground crew. This meant the ones who were still here at the gliding school were all at least three years younger than me. Most of them were eleven and twelve year olds still in primary school who itched to join the Luftwaffe as air force pilots some day. For now, they were all members of the Hitler Youth organisation.

Cousin Jonni was the boss. It was he who had told me about Hanna Reitsch, Germany's greatest test pilot. He had seen her flying over the stadium in Berlin at the Olympic Games in 1936 and said she was the finest pilot he'd ever seen.

Hanna Reitsch became my inspiration. I followed her daring adventures in the newspaper and on the radio. I started gliding just about the time Hanna Reitsch was awarded her Iron Cross Second Class medal for her services to Germany. From one of her stories of survival I learned to watch for soaring birds, as they'd show me air currents to safely lift my glider above the mountains.

I had burst into tears when I heard that Hanna Reitsch had nearly been killed in a crash trying to fly a rocket in 1942. I sent her a get-well card while she was in the hospital. I liked to think that maybe she had noticed it among the thousands of good wishes she got from all over Germany – surely my card was the only one from a young teenage girl who was also a glider pilot.

After that accident, Flight Captain Hanna Reitsch was awarded the Iron Cross First Class medal, the first and so far the only woman to have earned this honour. And she was only a civilian pilot, not even in the military! It was Hanna Reitsch's fame and skills that made Cousin Jonni willing to teach a girl to fly. If she could do it, so could I.

Sometimes a new student complained about me, a girl, being there at the Ulmenhain Gliding School, but the three older male instructors would laugh.

"Don't tell me you've never heard of Hanna Reitsch!" Cousin Jonni would say to the student. "If Germany's greatest test pilot is a woman, there's nothing wrong with Ingrid Hartman flying at the Ulmenhain Gliding School!"

Then they'd make that student take a trial flight with me.

Nothing stops a boy mocking you as fast as putting his life in your hands in the air. He might moan about it later, but he wouldn't ever question my abilities again.

Today, after my encounter with Region Leader Wulfsen, I felt nervous but also determined as I hiked up the steep, snowy lane that led to the small wooden lodge we called the clubhouse. This served as the gliding school's canteen and office.

I reached the airfield and saw a group of schoolboys taking turns launching and landing the three flimsy Schneider "school gliders". The boys on the ground stood watching those in the air, and everybody's breath came out in puffs of cloud.

I saluted and the boys saluted back.

"Heil Hitler!"

The boys did it without thinking.

Just like everywhere else, I was careful not to speak at the gliding school unless I really had to. I did not consider these boys, training for the military, to be my friends. The blue tits and sparrows at my bird table were more reliable. I didn't need to worry that the birds might report me for not giving the correct greeting.

But Cousin Jonni welcomed me. "Hello, Ingrid. You're just the person I was looking for! It's a perfect afternoon for soaring, but it's so cold I can't let the boys do anything other than take off and land in the school gliders. They keep pointing out that the Crane has an enclosed cockpit, but none of them are up to flying it without a safety pilot. My other instructors aren't here today because the weather's been so bad, and I need to stay on the ground to supervise the boys. Could you take one or two of them up in the Crane for a few short flights?"

I nodded in eager agreement. It was exactly the opening I needed. A "safety pilot"! After the boys had gone home, I'd ask Cousin Jonni if he could make that role into something more official, or at least more permanent.

In the meantime, the tension in my stomach relaxed a little at the prospect of being in the air.

CHAPTER 5

"Hey, boys, get the Crane out!" Cousin Jonni yelled. "Ingrid will take one of you aloft. Max, you can go first."

A handful of the boys started to clear the launching slope, pulling the small school gliders off to the side and getting the bungee rope ready to hook to the nose of the Crane. A couple of others slid the Crane aircraft out of the shed on its skid and began to direct it carefully by the wingtips across the snowy launching field.

To launch any of our gliders, we had to attach the middle of a big bungee rope to a ring in the nose of the aircraft. Five boys hung on to each end of the rope and ran forward across the snowy field until the bungee ends were pulled tight behind them. When they let go, the ring and rope fell away, and the glider catapulted into the sky. It took a team of us to do it – everyone working together as if we were flying an enormous kite.

I climbed into the Crane and strapped myself into the cockpit with Max in front of me. I was at peace with the world and perfectly at ease with myself in this small cocoon of fabric, wood and Perspex. In the sky, I was a thousand times more confident than I was on the ground – perhaps even happy, if I could admit to feeling happiness since my mother's death.

Even fearless.

My worries fell away as I pulled the canopy shut over my head.

"Heave!" shouted the boy in the front of the line.

Ahead of us, the group began to tug the launch rope across the snowy airfield.

"Double strength!" cried the boy.

I relaxed into the jolting bumps as the Crane skidded over the packed snow.

"*Away!*" the boy yelled.

There was another bump as the bungee rope released us, and the wonderful moment when the glider let go of the earth. In the air I lowered the

Crane's nose to pick up speed, then raised it to soar aloft.

Within moments, Max and I were over the roofs and steeples of Ulmenhain village, perfect and covered in white. It was like a scene in an Alpine souvenir snow globe.

"You c-c-can fly," I told Max, and let him take the controls. He turned towards the mountains to try to find an air current that would carry us higher.

"There," I said, and pointed towards a soaring hawk, remembering what Hanna Reitsch had said about watching the birds. The hawk would show us where the upward air currents were.

The air got colder as we climbed. My fingers and toes began to ache. The bitter and painful cold was the trade-off for being in this amazing bubble of freedom. I was among the mountains with my beautiful homeland spread beneath me under a dusting of fir and frost. In spite of the cold, there was no place I'd rather be than soaring up here, as high as the hawks and higher, safe in the air ...

Of course it was wartime, and so we were never really safe in the air. The danger was different to the danger I faced on the ground – but it was still there. I knew that. And as if to prove it, we suddenly spotted another plane up there with us.

"Look!" Max exclaimed, and pointed.

We often saw other planes – Messerschmitt fighters and fast new aircraft from the factory nearby sometimes came roaring over or under us in the sky. The planes were jet powered and top-secret projects, but they weren't so secret when you saw them sharing the sky. Everybody at the gliding school knew there was important war work going on in the factory less than a hundred kilometres away.

This plane didn't look like anything fast or new. It was a powered propeller aircraft, but it looked awkward and less aerodynamic than the sleek Crane we were flying.

I squinted at it for a moment and recognised its high wings and the gangling legs of its undercarriage. It was a Stork – not a fighter or a new design but a simple reconnaissance plane built for landing and taking off in a very short distance.

"I'll fly," I said to Max.

I glided down to get a closer look at the strange plane puttering slowly towards our village via the pass in the high mountains. We approached the Stork and saw the black cross of the Luftwaffe on its side, marking it as part of the German Air Force, and the black swastika of the Nazi government on its tail.

The strange Stork flew lower as it neared the landing field of our gliding school.

The reality of it hit me. A Luftwaffe reconnaissance plane landing at our remote Alpine airfield reminded me that out beyond the ring of mountains that protected us, people were fighting and dying. For some reason, this Stork was bringing the war to our village.

I found the downward current of air and glided towards the earth in a tight, spiralling turn. I didn't know what was going on, so I thought we should get back on the ground to find out.

"Are we landing so soon?" Max asked. "Can I fly the rest of the way?"

I let Max take the controls as we followed the strange plane back to the gliding school.

CHAPTER 6

The Luftwaffe pilot had landed the Stork ahead of us and was already standing on the snowy airfield by the time we'd glided back down to earth.

The pilot was a tall young man, fair haired, and he wore a warm flight suit with a fur collar. The schoolboys clustered around this air force pilot like bees around a rosebush – this was a real wartime hero who'd swooped to earth right at our feet!

The boys saluted him with stretched right arms and a chorus of "*Heil Hitler!*" The pilot returned the salute, nodding to them seriously. I saw one of them say something to him and point to the wooden clubhouse.

Then the air force pilot turned to look at me as I climbed out of the Crane glider. The tall young man could easily see over the heads of the admiring boys. His cheeks were red with cold, and he wasn't smiling. But that changed when he saw me, and he grinned and called out an old local greeting instead of the regulation "*Heil Hitler*".

"Ingrid! *Gruss Gott*, God's greetings!" the pilot said. "I should have known it was the Flying Mouse in the sky alongside me – no one else here descends in such fast, neat corkscrews!"

My heart leapt with joy as I recognised him. It was Emil Bruck, three years older than me, who'd started gliding at exactly the same time I had. He'd become my best friend when we were learning to fly, like a big brother. We'd kept up a joking competition about our achievements while we were students together, before he joined the Luftwaffe as an air force pilot on the day he turned eighteen. It was Emil's book by the French pilot that I'd been reading for the sixth time just that morning. *Wind, Sand and Stars* – the book that had been so absorbing I hadn't bothered to answer the door when a Nazi official hammered on it.

What a wonderful surprise it was to have Emil Bruck land at Ulmenhain at the end of this awful day!

Emil said to me, "The last time I saw you was in June, and you were wearing that wide straw hat with breadcrumbs scattered on the rim so the sparrows would sit on it. A feeding station for birds on your head!"

I could feel my cold cheeks start to heat up. Seeing Emil again wasn't just a lovely finish to a terrible day – it was the nicest thing that had happened for a long time. Emil stood there among the boys, with his tired eyes and his friendly greeting, and all my worries were replaced with the thoughts of the book I'd borrowed last summer and had read again and again. I had been longing to know what he thought of it himself.

Instead of returning Emil's greeting, I blurted out, "I've read your b-b-b-book five times. I'm reading it again right n-n-now."

For a moment Emil looked confused. Then he remembered and gave me another wide smile. "*Wind, Sand and Stars!* No one ever gives that back. Every pilot I know likes Saint-Exupéry's books about flying even better than Karl May's cowboy adventure stories!"

Emil strode across to the Crane and offered a hand to Max to help him climb out. He patted the boy on the back and said, "Did Ingrid let you take the controls for that landing? Nice work."

Max gulped and nodded, so full of admiration for this Luftwaffe hero that he couldn't make himself answer. I felt a tiny bit better – for once it wasn't me who was struggling to speak.

Blushing, Max hurried to join the safety of his friends, and Emil turned back to me. "What's your favourite part of *Wind, Sand and Stars?*" he asked.

I forgot everything else in the joy of being able to share my thoughts about Antoine de Saint-Exupéry with my friend.

"When Antoine lands his p-p-plane alone in ... in the Atlas Mountains," I said. "And ... and—"

"Oh yes, and he sees all the meteorites," remembered Emil. "And then he realises he's the first person ever to set foot there, and there is nothing between himself and the stars."

I nodded. I'd forgotten how much of a talker Emil was.

"The part I like is when Antoine crashes in the desert and goes mad from thirst," said Emil, "and when the desert nomad gives him water. And then he's so grateful that he feels that all his friends and enemies are merged into this one man who is letting him drink, and he has no enemy left in all the world. That's the part I like: not the loneliness of the mountains but the joy of human beings coming together. And he says, 'We need to drink, but also we need to communicate'."

Emil glanced backwards, checking that he was out of earshot of the boys. Then he lowered his voice and added, "I'm so grateful I'm a reconnaissance pilot and not a fighter pilot. I just got lucky, I suppose – but I don't have to shoot down other planes or drop bombs. I get to take pictures and deliver messages. I'm doing important war work *and* I'm helping people to communicate."

I bit my lip, nodding. I understood. Then I had a desperate, excited idea. Doing communication flights for the Luftwaffe would be even more useful to Germany than training glider pilots. If Hanna Reitsch could do it, maybe I could too.

"Is there … is there air work like that a g-g-girl can do? Like Hanna Reitsch?" I asked.

"Hanna Reitsch is a test pilot, not a reconnaissance pilot," Emil pointed out. "I don't think you have the experience to be a test pilot."

"B-b-but Hanna Reitsch also flies …" I paused and took a breath, preparing myself for the difficult word I wanted to say. "She flies on prop … propaganda missions, at rallies, to encourage p-p-people, and her air shows are a kind of communication too."

Emil laughed. "I suppose they are," he agreed. "Is the Flying Mouse going to become the next Hanna Reitsch?"

"I'm ... I'm serious," I said. "I need to use my flight skills or I'm in d-d-danger of ..." I trailed off. I couldn't tell Emil what the real danger was. I couldn't tell anyone.

I turned to busy myself with the Crane glider, getting behind one wing to start to push it back towards the shed. It moved easily over the snow on its skid, but Emil got behind the other wing to help me. After a moment, he said in his friendly way, "You know, I have met Hanna Reitsch – my commander is working on a project with her. If I see her again, I'll mention that you might be able to assist her."

The heat came back into my cheeks. I glanced over at Emil – he was looking at me with bright eyes as he waited to see what my reaction would be.

You had to be *so careful* about what you said to people. And I had to be more careful than anyone. Was Emil testing me? Or just teasing me? Did he really want to help, and could he really put my name forward?

I was willing to take that chance. It might be the chance of a lifetime.

"Thank you, Emil," I said as we pushed the Crane glider over the snow together. "And, oh ... I must give you back your b-b-book."

"Keep it," Emil said. "I've had to replace *Wind, Sand and Stars* three times – it's my Air Group's most popular book about flying. I always have two copies around just so I have an extra one to lend to people."

Emil didn't say anything else about Hanna Reitsch.

Cousin Jonni came out of the clubhouse to see what was going on. He recognised Emil.

"Captain Emil Bruck! Our own war hero!" Jonni cried.

"I can't stay," Emil said. "I've been sent to take photographs of an American bomber that our fighters shot down in the mountains. I think there are survivors, so I landed here to make a telephone call from your clubhouse, which will be faster than flying back to deliver the message in that damned slow Stork. I'll call from here, but then I've got to return to my airbase before it gets dark."

"Of course!" Cousin Jonni said, bowing. "Ingrid, take Captain Bruck up to the clubhouse, get him a hot drink and write up his landing in the visiting aircraft log. I'll get the boys to clear the airfield for the Stork to take off again."

"Hot drinks and an entry in the visitor's log!" exclaimed Emil. "It's like landing at a ski resort. I will tell all my friends." He turned to smile at me. "*All* of them," he said with emphasis. "If anyone important ever lands in Ulmenhain, maybe the Flying Mouse here can give an air show as well as make coffee!"

I knew that Emil would keep his word about recommending me to Hanna Reitsch.

PART 2: The Stork

CHAPTER 7

Cousin Jonni agreed to my father's suggestion of calling me a "junior instructor". He helped find reasons for me to spend more time at the Ulmenhain Gliding School, even when there wasn't any flying going on: sweeping and scrubbing, rationing refreshments, filling in the logbooks and ledgers, searching the forest slopes for firewood.

The clubhouse was up a long, steep icy lane that a car would find impossible until spring. I hiked that hill before dawn every morning, coming back down just after sunset, hoping that I wouldn't attract any more attention from Nazi Party officials if I didn't get in their way. I didn't think Region Leader Wulfsen was the sort of person who'd want to march a mile and a half up that lane in the snow to track down a mouse of a girl who'd failed to let him in her house politely, but you never knew. He could always send someone else if he was that angry.

*

In March, another Luftwaffe Stork arrived at Ulmenhain. But this one wasn't flown by my friend Emil.

Most of the young glider students still attended the primary school in the village, so on weekdays there weren't many air launches at the gliding school until school finished at noon. I often spent the mornings there all by myself, and I was alone when the second Stork arrived. I was busy with the Crane, repairing the flaking paint and checking the bolts. It was delicate work, and cold too, because I had to do it without gloves.

I looked up at the sound of the strange engine. I could see the small Stork plane puttering along the valley. When it began to make a steep descent, I stood up to watch. The Stork headed into the wind and powered down to land at the end of our airfield. Then it came rumbling across the packed snow until it was close to the clubhouse, where the engine stopped.

The pilot threw open the door of the plane. Inside the cockpit I saw a small and feminine person, wrapped up in flying gear. She hopped down lightly beneath the Stork's high wings and came walking across the field towards me.

She carried a pillow in one hand and pulled off her pilot's leather helmet with the other, revealing a red and blue woolly cap below it. She had the face of a china doll, with wide blue eyes and pink cheeks, a perky tilted nose and a child's smile. In a second I recognised the young woman from the newspaper clippings I'd saved – this was Flight Captain Hanna Reitsch herself, the record-breaking test pilot.

She was walking towards me over the packed snow and waving her helmet.

"*Heil Hitler!*" I called carefully in greeting, and was thankful that I didn't stutter.

Hanna Reitsch returned the salute with a smile, then called out, "Is that Ingrid Hartman?"

She knew my name!

I nodded, but I didn't dare try to say anything else.

Hanna laughed. My mouth must have been gaping. She reached me and pulled off her gloves so she could shake my bare hand.

CHAPTER 8

Hanna Reitsch was a tiny woman, shorter than me. The pillow was for her to sit on in the cockpit, to raise her so she could see out. There were faint scars on her pretty face, and I remembered the card I'd sent her after her crash last year. Had Emil really managed to mention me to her?

I held my breath, waiting for her to speak.

"Ingrid, I'm so pleased to meet you," Hanna Reitsch said. "I've heard so much about you from your friend, Captain Emil Bruck! He called you the Flying Mouse." Saying that name made her laugh again. "I'd like to talk to your head instructor."

I shook my head. "He's n-n-not here ..."

I remembered the mess I'd made when I failed to talk to Region Leader Wulfsen. I didn't want to embarrass myself in front of my hero, Hanna Reitsch.

"He will be in s-s-soon," I said. I let out my breath in a rush and rubbed at my fingers, covered in chilblains from working in the cold. They were sore and burning, so I knew I was wide awake and not lost in a dream. Hanna must be cold, too – it would have been even colder several thousand feet in the air than it was on the ground. "Come get a hot … a hot drink," I suggested.

Our cabin clubhouse wasn't much warmer than outside, because we didn't want to waste fuel by keeping a fire burning in the stove. I only lit the fire for a short time just before dawn so I could boil water and get the place ready for the day's flying. I hurried to pour Hanna a cup of fake coffee from the flask that I prepared each morning.

"This is the best barley and acorn coffee I've ever tasted!" Hanna said. "Is it perhaps an old family recipe?"

I couldn't help smiling. "Yes, it is," I said. "My g-g-grandmother's." I wanted to tell her it was a recipe from the Great War and that it had been passed down through three generations, but I didn't think I could explain all that without stuttering.

"So you can cook as well as fly!" Hanna said, and laughed. "Be faithful, be pure, be German. That's what I told the League of German Girls when

I gave my speech to them last year after I got out of hospital. It's just as good advice for an audience of one as it is for an audience of two thousand! Do the best that you can. Everyone is working so hard for the country, and everyone wants to do more, don't they?"

Hanna was warming her hands around the tin cup I'd given to her. Over the brim of the cup her eyes sparkled, gazing right into mine. I wasn't sure what she was talking about, but she was the most enchanting person I'd ever met.

Under her spell, I dared to ask, "Is there m-m-more that I can do?"

After a moment, Hanna put down her cup and reached into her flight bag. From out of a cardboard folder, she took a handful of photographs showing pictures of a glider in flight. "Look, it's you!"

Hanna spread the photos on the clubhouse table. They were a wonderful sequence taken from the air, showing a Crane glider turning gracefully against a backdrop of mountains. It only took me a second to recognise the landscape surrounding Ulmenhain.

"Your friend Emil Bruck took these pictures of your Crane just before he landed here last month," Hanna continued. "I met him at a strategy meeting, and he showed me these photos among some others he had for us. He mentioned Ulmenhain and how much you love gliding, and I remembered that you sent me a get-well card while I was in the hospital last year."

So she had noticed my card! My smile grew so wide that my cheeks began to hurt.

"I've been asked to do a propaganda tour," Hanna told me. "I'll be giving speeches to our new pilots – young men not much older than you who are just beginning their training with the Luftwaffe. We want to recruit a few top glider pilots, and I want to impress them with some tricks they might not have learned in training. I thought it would be fun to have another girl come along with me."

My heart pounded. Could Hanna possibly mean *me*? Why else would she have come here?

Hanna went on, "I'm looking for an assistant. Someone like me – charming and talented! Your friend Emil assured me that the Flying Mouse was up to the job. Would you like to join me?"

But something about this wonderful proposal made me hesitate.

Giving speeches?

I couldn't do it. Not even for the marvellous Flight Captain Hanna Reitsch. I met her eyes, but I shook my head without saying anything.

She laughed. "Oh, I'll be the one making the speeches," she added. "Emil warned me that you're not much of a talker. But I love talking – I love a good audience! I want to give our boys a bit of an air show so that they'll understand I'm really one of them, not just a pretty face! And I thought it would be more exciting for them if there were *two* of us in the air at the same time. We'll be in Hawk gliders. Have you ever flown a Hawk? No? You'll love it! It's like dancing in the sky. I'll give you a few hours' training and we'll practise together before we go on tour."

Hanna took another sip of the fake coffee, then continued.

"I want someone working with me who really understands gliders," she explained. "I need someone whose flight skills are more advanced than the new pilots in the audience, but not so much that they'll be intimidated. You and I can show off together. They're all in awe of me, but you're closer to their skill set, so they'll feel they can learn to do it too. And a young woman in the air is a rarity – they'll love it! All you have to do is come along on the tour and sit in on my lectures, smile sweetly at the young pilots and write down their names, and then follow me in the air. Do you think you can do that?"

Hanna's offer seemed as magical as if she were a genie who'd turned up to grant me my greatest wish.

"I've only got these pictures, and your friend's word, to prove that you're a decent glider pilot," Hanna said. "So if you don't mind, I'd like to run a test flight with you here. If I'm satisfied, you can come with me. But only if your people here can spare you, of course. I won't let you come without your parents' permission."

"My m-m-mother died last year," I said. "But my father ..."

I hesitated as my heart sank. I had never mentioned to my father the possibility of flying with Hanna Reitsch. What if he was afraid to let me go? What if he wouldn't let me take the job? I couldn't leave without my father's blessing.

"I can fly ..." I said, and drew a deep breath. "The instructors will arrive in half an hour, and I c-c-can fly for you as s-s-soon as they get here."

If I could prove myself in the air, maybe Flight Captain Hanna Reitsch would be willing to talk to my father for me.

CHAPTER 9

"Flight Captain Reitsch!" cried Cousin Jonni half an hour later after he and the other instructors had all shaken hands with our wonderful visitor. "Germany's greatest test pilot! What an honour to have you land here at Ulmenhain! I saw your air display at the Olympics in 1936 – you were superb then, even before they awarded you with two Iron Crosses! But you want to take Ingrid away from us? I am not surprised – Ingrid is the best student I've ever had."

I felt as if my whole face were going red, right to the tips of my ears. Cousin Jonni had told me I was a good glider pilot, but he had never said I was the best student he ever had.

"I want to see Ingrid do a test flight first," Hanna said. "On my propaganda tour, there will be two display aircraft, and the other pilot will have to follow me the way a fighter pilot follows his flight leader. I need to be sure Ingrid will be able to keep up with me and make her own piloting decisions. Right now, I'd like to see her take off solo in one of the Schneider school gliders. That's what most of the new pilots will be used to flying, and I want to see how Ingrid's performance compares to theirs."

Hanna turned and spoke to me directly. "When you're in the air, I'll meet you in the Stork, and you can line up behind me. Try to keep a space of ten wingspans between us, and then just follow me and do what I do."

Cousin Jonni and I led Hanna out to the shed where the school gliders were kept. My heart was hammering like an aircraft engine. I wanted to pass this test more than I'd ever wanted anything in my life – but I knew it was going to be a challenge in more ways than one.

A school glider had no cockpit. It was like sitting on a ski with wings. It's true that it was very stable and easy to fly, but there wasn't a thing between you and the elements. You were there in the sky with the wind against your entire body, and the higher you soared, the colder it got. It got one degree centigrade colder for every 150 metres that you climbed. If it was minus five on the ground when you took off, it would be minus fifteen once you'd soared to 1,500 metres. You were numb with cold when you landed.

But if the hawks and eagles could endure it, surely I could too.

Half a dozen eager young glider pupils arrived just after noon, and with Cousin Jonni and the two regular instructors they made a team to launch my glider. I sat on my winged ski waiting to take flight.

"Heave!" Cousin Jonni yelled.

The gliding school staff and students all ran ahead of me with the bungee rope over their shoulders.

"Double strength!" Jonni shouted.

The bungee rope shook with tension.

"*Away!*" Jonni finished.

The skid beneath me lifted easily off the packed snow and I was in the air in seconds. I found a swirl of wind, eased the control stick back and began to climb.

I could hear the engine of the Stork as Hanna took off and puttered up behind me. I climbed in circles, nearly silently. The school glider's fabric wings made only as much noise as the sail of a yacht, so I could tell where Hanna was just by listening for her engine.

She passed beneath me in a straight line as I spiralled upwards. As I looked, I saw the Stork below me just the way a bird might see it.

Hanna positioned her plane in front of mine and dipped her wings – a signal for me to follow her. She was a glider pilot herself and knew that I couldn't control my aircraft's climb with power the way she could in the Stork. But I knew these mountain winds the way I knew the backs of my own hands, and I was able to keep up with her.

We soared together up the narrow valley south of Ulmenhain into the Alps.

*

The first challenge came without warning as we approached Lake Plansee. No one from the gliding school was allowed to fly here any more, because the government had converted the hotel on its shores into a prison last year. But Hanna flew straight over the forbidden area. As she crossed the lake, she suddenly began to dive steeply towards its icy white surface.

Hanna was using all the power the Stork's engine could give her – I could hear it. I didn't have power, so I couldn't dive as fast, but I could dive just as steeply. I sped down after her, the icy wind cutting into my flight suit and woollen padding.

Suddenly the Stork in front of me began to climb, making an elegant curve in the air.

Hanna was looping the loop in a Luftwaffe reconnaissance plane.

It didn't look to me like the kind of plane you could loop in. It was built for short take-offs and landings, not aerobatics. And using power like that burns a lot of fuel, which was wasteful. She probably wasn't supposed to be doing it, even for fun. But that's what she was doing – and I was supposed to copy every move she made.

I didn't have the speed or height to loop the loop in the school glider. But I was up to proving my skill. Keeping a safe distance, I pushed my aircraft more steeply into the dive, until the surface of the icy lake seemed to be rushing at me like an oncoming avalanche. I pulled up, judging the wind, and climbed skyward again. Now all I could see was sky.

I waited until my small aircraft was standing on its tail in the air, then I let it fall back into a natural glide. That was as close as I could come to a loop right now.

I'd lost height. I couldn't keep up with the Stork. If I wasn't careful, I would have to land on the frozen surface of the lake. I had to find an updraft so I could soar once more.

I had no way of knowing whether I'd passed or failed that part of my test. I hadn't actually flown a loop, as Hanna had done, nor had I been able to keep up with her. But I couldn't even sob with disappointment – it was too hard to breathe in this high, cold air.

CHAPTER 10

Hanna circled back again to join my small school glider in the air above Lake Plansee.

Once more, she rocked the Stork's wings to let me know she could see me and to tell me to follow her. Now we began to climb along the upwind side of the Zugspitze, Germany's highest mountain outside Austria. It towered nearly 3,000 metres above sea level.

Both Emil and Cousin Jonni had told Flight Captain Hanna Reitsch that I was a talented glider pilot, and that was true. But I was no daredevil, and I was not stupid. I had only ever scaled the snow-capped heights of the Zugspitze on summer days. I treated the unpredictable mountain winds with respect, and in the unprotected school glider I knew that I risked frostbite as well as oxygen deprivation if I wasn't careful.

Hanna was in a sealed cockpit in her Stork. She was protected from the elements. And if she was caught in a downdraft, she could use her engine to help her climb away from the bare and lifeless slopes of rock and ice. I could not.

But she'd told me to follow her: it was a test.

Higher and higher we spiralled up the peak. My cheeks were numb, even beneath the soft moleskin mask I wore to protect my face. Frost furred the edges of my goggles, making it feel as if I was slowly going blind. I flexed my fingers against the controls. If I couldn't see and I couldn't feel, I wouldn't be able to fly. But I could hear the Stork's engine purring ahead of me, and I could see its black shape against the Zugspitze's snowy crags.

Suddenly Hanna changed direction and began to fly straight towards the rocky mountainside.

I followed her.

I thought then that if she flew right into the mountain and crashed, I would follow her to destruction.

She didn't crash. At the last possible second, she veered away, increased the power of her engine and zoomed steeply down and away from the mountainside.

But I couldn't complete the same move using power the way she'd done it.

I clenched my teeth. My face was so cold I couldn't feel my jaw. If I hesitated one more second, I'd be dead.

I stood the glider on its wingtip in the air, as if I were falling out of a half-loop, turning like a spinning coin. Then I pushed the nose forward into a plunge. As I turned, I couldn't see the terrain beneath me – if the mountainside was uneven, I'd hit it so hard in my dive that I'd be killed instantly.

But I was lucky – or maybe Hanna had chosen that sheer slope on purpose, knowing what I'd have to do to save myself. I shot 200 metres downwards until I was able to ease up the nose of the school glider and level out.

Where was the Stork? I peered around through my iced-up goggles. I listened. There it was, a black shape below me – the distance between us had grown.

Now that I'd escaped death, I was warm from the rush of adrenaline. I wasn't going to let Hanna get away from me. I pushed the school glider into another dive down the mountainside, picking up speed as I descended so that I could catch up with her.

Hanna flew slowly back to the gliding school, waiting for me to catch the right air currents. Her flying seemed calm and patient now.

The test must be over.

Hanna landed ahead of me. She leapt out of her plane and joined Cousin Jonni and the others as they came running across the field to meet me.

"Aren't you wonderful, Ingrid?!" Hanna cried aloud.

I was so stiff with cold I couldn't undo my own straps.

"Nearly as wonderful as me," Hanna laughed. "You'll do. If you can fly a school glider like that, imagine what you'll be able to do with a Hawk! Let's go and inspire the troops together."

She reached out to undo my straps and smiled at me.

"Are you ready to ask your father's permission?" she said. "There's no time to waste. I'd like to take you with me when I leave Ulmenhain this afternoon."

I nodded. I was ready to follow her anywhere.

CHAPTER 11

Cousin Jonni came along with me and Hanna to talk to my father. My father didn't try to stop me, not against the three of us. He listened seriously to Cousin Jonni's praise and Hanna's passion. Then he nodded wearily. I hadn't seen my father so grey-faced and defeated since the awful moment last year when he'd stood up and walked away from my mother's bedside after she had finally died.

"You may take Ingrid with you," my father said to Hanna at last. "But keep her in the air and don't let her try to speak to anyone."

Minna, our housekeeper, shed a few tears as she hugged me goodbye and put hot potatoes into my pockets for the journey. My father stood at the bottom of the stairs in the hall, watching silently. He looked as if he were about to turn and run up the stairs two at a time to get back to his dark study. He looked as if he couldn't wait to get this moment over with.

I knew that my father was a loving, kind man underneath his stiff formality. I couldn't quite bring myself to try to hug him, but I held out my hand. He took it and we shook hands solemnly, looking each other in the eye. My father nodded. Suddenly he laid his other hand on top, so that his two hands were clasped around mine, engulfing it in a firm and warm embrace.

"Till we meet again, Ingrid," he said.

I wondered if that would ever happen. I knew that because of the war, this might be the last time my father and I ever saw each other. I would be closer than ever to danger as I flew with Hanna, travelling to Luftwaffe airbases to give displays to young Luftwaffe pilots, risking becoming a target for enemy bombs.

"Don't worry about m-m-me," I said. "This is my chance to d-d-do some good for Germany. What could be more p-p-patriotic than encouraging young air force pilots?"

*

I followed Hanna to the Stork that we were going to fly away in and realised that for the first time I would be in the sky in a Luftwaffe aircraft – a plane belonging to the German Air Force.

The cramped rear passenger seat of the Stork was cold, but compared to the unprotected school glider, the small enclosed cabin seemed luxurious. I watched my village drop away from me for the last time. My body was still stiff and numb, but my heart and mind were racing with excitement.

At last I was going to do something real to help with the war – and I was leaving behind the intense fear and uncertainty that I'd been living with ever since Region Leader Wulfsen's visit. From now on, I would be flying for Germany. I would be serving my country, not living in fear of its officials.

I have no enemy left in all the world, I thought, recalling Emil's favourite passage from *Wind, Sand and Stars*. That's how I felt now.

Oh! I realised suddenly that I'd left Emil's book next to my bed. How I would miss Antoine de Saint-Exupéry's flight adventures!

I comforted myself with the thought that now I would be living my *own* flight adventures.

Then I turned away from Ulmenhain and looked over Hanna's shoulder at the open sky ahead of me.

PART 3: The Parasite

CHAPTER 12

It was late in March 1944 when I joined Hanna and we set off on her propaganda tour, visiting airfields where new pilots were training. We stayed in elegant guest houses where I was mostly given a room to myself. We would be driven by an officer along city streets ruined by enemy bombs to get to our guest house from a new airfield. We'd pass through areas where the homes and shops had been destroyed, then pull up in the neat driveway of a grand house that had somehow survived the air raids. It was a strange contrast to get used to – seeing so much suffering from inside an officer's private car, but never getting close to it.

Often my bedroom window looked out over a stable courtyard much like ours back in Ulmenhain. I could see house sparrows fluttering in and out of the roof, and for a moment I would ache with loneliness for the flocks of familiar bird-friends I'd left behind for this odd new life. Every now and then I got a chance to slip away into some stranger's garden and I would just stand there watching the birds.

But most of the time I was too busy to feel homesick.

I was given a uniform, a wonderful thing, as if I were a real air force *Helferin*, a Luftwaffe helper. Even Hanna didn't have a uniform – she made up her own, wearing a smart black dress with white piping and her Iron Cross First Class medal when she wanted to impress people. She didn't have a real military rank, either – "Flight Captain" was an honorary civilian title.

I didn't have any title. I didn't even get a salary, though I didn't have to pay for anything. But the Luftwaffe made me sign a contract that swore me to secrecy.

*

There was one thing about Hanna that made her terrifying to work with, and it wasn't that she was a daredevil pilot. It was that she trusted *everybody*. Hanna couldn't see the dark side of anybody, or of any situation. She was almost stupid with it. She'd made me believe that my job with her would be performing as part of a glider team, flying in propaganda air shows to encourage new Luftwaffe pilots. That was true, but it wasn't the whole story. These new pilots would be signing up for a dark and secret mission.

Hanna explained this secret mission to me before my first flight in the Hawk glider I'd be flying with her in our air shows. Perhaps she felt she could trust me simply because I hardly ever spoke. I'd only been recommended by Emil Bruck and Cousin Jonni after all. But on that first day, she gave me information that I could have been killed for if I'd passed it on.

"I'm in charge of forming a new flight group," Hanna told me. "It will be named the Leonidas Squadron, after the king of Sparta who died fighting against the Persians at the battle of Thermopylae. A fight to the death is what we're facing if we want to win this war, and I call this mission 'Operation Self-Sacrifice'. The Leonidas Squadron will be a suicide group, performing a suicide mission."

She spoke seriously but not dramatically. I could hardly believe what I was hearing – not just about the awful mission she wanted our young pilots to perform, but also the way she spoke of it so bluntly and frankly. It was as if she were simply warning me to be careful of turbulent air when I tried out the Hawk glider for the first time. Wasn't she horrified by her own idea – *a suicide mission?*

Perhaps Hanna's ease with words and her adoring crowds had turned her into my exact opposite – someone who never worried *at all* about what she was going to say.

"We need to destroy enemy battleships in an accurate and efficient manner," Hanna went on. "I want to recruit talented young pilots who are willing to fly gliders loaded with bombs straight into the sea beneath a battleship. It's going to be a challenge because we can't tell the pilots what they'll be doing until we're sure they're committed to the mission and to its secrecy. So you and I will give these young men a good show to raise their spirits, and I'll give them a stirring speech and ask for the bravest of them to interview with me. You can also deal with the sign-up sheets and arrange the interviews."

Suddenly I understood exactly how my mother must have felt as the awful new rules were introduced at the Ulmenhain Youth Hospital. Each new regulation made by our government and each new plan for winning the war seemed to lead to more killing and more death. But even if I tried to back out now, where would I go? Would I return to Ulmenhain as a failure, a quitter? That would *surely* attract the attention of the regional Nazi propaganda office.

All I have to do is fly a Hawk glider in an air show, I reminded myself. *And write down names and appointment times on a sign-up sheet.*

I could do this for Germany, couldn't I?

Of course I could. It wasn't what my mother had faced when she was told to neglect helpless children who didn't know what was happening. Hanna's recruits would be young men who knew what they were signing up for and were responsible for themselves.

I could do it.

And I thought I *had* to do it – even if I didn't like it.

CHAPTER 13

Hanna's rallies turned sensible young men into roaring crowds. Her performances reminded me of the newsreels I'd seen of the Führer. What a speaker Hanna was! She knew just how to get people excited, and she was good at it. She always came rushing in after everyone sat down, as if she were late. She'd wave and grin as she made her way to the front of the canvas tent that had been erected for her lecture.

"*Heil Hitler!* Hello! Hello! How wonderful to see all of you here!" Hanna exclaimed at the very first rally. "Are you excited about joining the Air Force? The Luftwaffe, the German Air Force, is the most powerful in the world, with the most amazing new planes – and you'll be flying them soon!"

Hanna climbed up to stand on a packing crate so that the people at the back of the tent could see her. She wore her formal black dress with her pilot's wings and her Iron Cross First Class medal. Everyone leaned forward eagerly to get a better view.

"You're the hope of our nation, all of you," Hanna told them warmly. "We're all heroes in the making – all willing to die for our country! But we want to win the war with as little loss of life as we can. Who wouldn't want to attack an enemy destroyer without harming civilians? Or fly into an enemy airbase and destroy their aircraft on the ground while avoiding killing innocent people? Think how many lives could be saved with just a few carefully planned air strikes – think how fast we could stop hostilities! It might end in our own deaths – we all know that every soldier signs a contract with death. But which of us wouldn't want our own deaths to end the dying for other people? Imagine if we were able to do that."

A serious silence fell in the lecture tent as they imagined it. No one there was more than five years older than me, apart from a row of half a dozen commanding officers standing at the back.

Hanna hadn't exactly told the pilots about the suicide mission – she hadn't told them that she was talking about a real operation being planned by the Luftwaffe, as she'd explained to me. But she'd come close enough to the truth to put the idea of heroic self-sacrifice into some of their heads.

Hanna gave her warm, beaming smile, holding out her arms. "You are all patriots," she continued, "and you are all here because you want to fly. I am making a list of recruits for the most dangerous of missions, so we'll be ready when the Luftwaffe needs us. Ingrid and I will take your names after the air display, and I will interview you over the next few days. Before that, let's show you what a pair of gliders can do!"

She climbed down from the packing crate and beckoned to me.

I stood up. My cheeks began to burn as I walked to the front of the tent to stand beside Hanna. But she did the speaking for me.

"This is Ingrid Hartman," Hanna told the crowd of young men. "She's had exactly the same training as you and is as confident in the air. But because she's a woman, she'll never be asked to risk her life for her country. All that she can do is inspire you. So come and watch our battling Hawks!"

I was almost desperate to get away from the curious stares of the young pilots and up into the familiar empty sky. There I would be confident and safe at the controls of the Hawk glider I had just learned to fly.

I smiled sweetly and said nothing, then followed Germany's greatest test pilot into the air.

Afterwards, I took names and arranged interviews for the young pilots who were already eager to commit their lives to the Leonidas Squadron. The thought that I was helping encourage them to their deaths made my heart ache. It was like an ugly crack in the shiny glass of my new Luftwaffe career.

CHAPTER 14

"Let me show you the new planes I've been flying," Hanna said to me casually a couple of days later. She spoke as if they weren't the most carefully guarded weapons of the Nazi government.

We were visiting Augsburg, the enormous airfield and Messerschmitt factory where the new aircraft were launched. We were less than a hundred kilometres from Ulmenhain, so close to home that in the air I could see the familiar shape of the Zugspitze mountain in the distance.

Hanna beckoned me into the hangar as our gliders were unpacked from the flatbed lorries they travelled in. Inside the hangar, aircraft in strange new shapes sat waiting like wild beasts to roar into our war-torn skies and defend us.

Hanna led me to a screened-off area in the back of the hangar and spoke to the soldiers on guard there with earnest charm. They let us through.

Now we were standing in front of one of the Luftwaffe's new secret aircraft.

It was very small – its wings were smaller even than one of the Schneider school gliders. But it had an engine that looked like a flame-thrower, mounted on top of its bullet-shaped body. I'd never seen anything like it, but it reminded me of the jet engines on our nation's deadly new planes called Swallows. I'd seen them screaming down the Alpine valleys on their test flights before they went into production.

"I hoped so much they'd let my Leonidas Squadron pilots fly this aircraft," Hanna said, rubbing its nose fondly as if it were a horse. "But no one agrees with me, because it was designed to fly without a pilot, and when they adjusted one so it could be tested with a pilot, no one but me was able to handle it. It's a flying bomb. It gets launched from a firing ramp, or is launched in flight from another aircraft. It's supposed to fly towards the enemy under its own power and then explode. Because it isn't guided, it can fly in bad weather when other aircraft can't, and it flies so fast that enemy pilots won't be able to shoot it down."

"What is it c-c-called?" I asked.

"It's a Fieseler Fi-103," Hanna told me. "Our number-one vengeance weapon, designed by the same man who designed the Stork! We call it a Cherry Stone because it drops like a cherry stone when it falls. Some call it a Doodlebug because of the buzzing noise the new pulse-jet engine makes in flight. You can hear it from fifteen kilometres away."

I nodded. I realised that I may not have seen one of these things before, but I was pretty sure I'd heard them echoing down the mountainsides on distant test flights.

Hanna sighed and continued. "It's not very accurate without a pilot to guide it – all you can do is point it in the direction you want it to go and hope for the best, and it drops like a bomb when the fuel runs out. That's what it's designed to do, of course! It can fly just fine with a lot of power behind it, but it glides about as well as a piano. Many good test pilots have been injured or even killed while flying it, so the Luftwaffe think we need to use a different aircraft for the Leonidas Squadron."

The whole time Hanna was speaking, I felt as if I too was dropping through space like a cherry stone.

Her hope was that this strange and sinister aircraft would carry brave young pilots to their death – and cause the deaths of others too. Again my heart ached at the thought of those eager boys my own age climbing into a cockpit they would never climb out of.

Also, I didn't want to know the Luftwaffe's strategy for winning the war. I knew I could be executed for knowing too much.

Hanna didn't seem to notice my discomfort. She beckoned me, moving within the gloom of the hangar to another aircraft. "Since the Leonidas Squadron won't be allowed to fly Doodlebugs, we've come up with another solution. Look at this."

I followed Hanna miserably. She stopped in front of another deadly looking but tiny plane, hardly any bigger than the Doodlebug flying bomb.

"Here's our secret weapon," Hanna said. "The Messerschmitt Me-328 parasite plane."

CHAPTER 15

The Me-328 parasite plane was smaller than a school glider, like the Doodlebug. It had an enclosed cockpit, but its wings were half the size of a school glider. I couldn't believe that Hanna expected to win the war flying this tiny plane.

"A parasite plane rides on the back of a larger bomber plane to the combat site and launches in flight," Hanna explained to me. "It's perfect for our mission – it's silent, stable in the air and easy to fly. With a good pilot at the controls, it will be an accurate and deadly glider bomb."

"Why are you t-t-telling me all these secrets?" I asked.

"I'd like you to try flying this plane," Hanna said in her friendly way.

"*M-me?!*" I gasped.

All along, Hanna had wanted my help because I had the same flight experience as the young men who'd have to take this plane into combat. She wanted me to test planes before they flew them.

Suddenly I properly understood her work as a test pilot. Day after day, Hanna risked her own life so that our new aircraft would be as safe and efficient as they could be *before* they were flown by pilots of the Luftwaffe. Hanna's work was as dangerous as flying into battle, and even less predictable.

And truthfully, I was *thrilled*. This was my chance to fly a new Luftwaffe secret weapon. Would this be the beginning of a career for me as a test pilot like Hanna herself? This made the dangerous knowledge I now had worthwhile. My heartache for the young Luftwaffe pilots didn't go away, but I accepted the dangerous secrets as a fair exchange for the chance to fly this plane. After all, I was good at keeping secrets.

"You've got the same capabilities as the new Leonidas Squadron pilots," Hanna said. "I'd like to be able to encourage the men we choose to fly by letting them know that you're able to fly this plane too."

"I ... I've never... never air-launched a g-g-glider—" I kept talking, ignoring my stutter. I knew by now that it didn't bother Hanna anyway. "We always g-g-g-ground-launch at Ulmenhain."

Hanna laughed as if it were nothing.

"You won't have to do anything until you're already 4,000 metres in the air," she said. "You'll be able to release the plane yourself – it's not hard. The aircraft that carries you up is a Dornier Do-217 bomber. I'll be on the ground watching, ready to meet you when you land. I want you to simulate an attack. You'll have to do a precision landing, but you won't know the spot until take-off. You'll have to find your way there yourself after you separate from the Dornier."

Hanna gave me her warm and winning smile. "Are you ready for this?" she asked.

I wondered whether Hanna had been given permission to use me as a test pilot because her superiors didn't want to waste any young men with similar skills.

But I nodded and smiled back.

*

My joy was mixed with nerves as I prepared for my first launched flight in the Me-328. I was seated in the tiny plane, and it was mounted on top of a Dornier bomber. It was exactly like a parasite, taking advantage of the larger plane's power and speed. I didn't have to do anything other than sit there wondering how I'd find the landing point later, while the huge bomber rumbled beneath me into the sky. As the Dornier took off, I watched the needle of the Me-328's altimeter turning around and around the dial as we rose higher and higher: 1,000 metres, 2,000, 3,000 ...

In my head, I imagined the boys of the Ulmenhain Gliding School running ahead of me. *Heave! Double strength!*

The altimeter needle pointed to 4,000 metres.

Away!

I took a deep breath of cold thin air and released the catch that connected my small parasite glider to the enormous bomber plane below me.

Then I was alone in the sky in an Me-328 Luftwaffe fighter plane.

Hanna was right about the tiny aircraft handling nicely – it was like wearing a flying suit. In a school glider, you were always aware of its huge sail-like wing creaking and flapping above you. In the Me-328, you didn't even feel the wind. You could steer it by shifting your weight. It was wonderful.

Once I was in the sky alone, the most difficult thing was finding my way from the icy thin air at 4,000 metres back to the landing spot. This was a line of camouflaged lorries in a farmer's field, meant to imitate the "battleships" that the Leonidas Squadron would have to attack.

It took me a bit longer than I'd hoped. Or perhaps I lingered a bit longer in the sky than I should have, if I am honest. I was thrilled to be alone in this amazing new and secret aircraft, so high above Germany that I could see the Baltic Sea – a dark strip of navy blue on the horizon. Wasn't I *lucky*?!

I landed right alongside the lorries. They would have been blown to pieces if I'd had a bomb attached to my small plane.

I pushed open the cockpit of the Me-328, and Hanna came running to meet me with her arms stretched out, all smiles. The fact I was able to land that plane with accuracy on my first try made Hanna even more eager to find recruits for Operation Self-Sacrifice.

She put in an order for a thousand of the new Me-328 aircraft to be built for the Leonidas Squadron's use. Hanna hoped that the first planes would be ready by the end of April.

CHAPTER 16

"I am volunteering as a pilot for the manned glider bomb," read the pledge. It was what the Leonidas Squadron volunteers had to sign once they'd passed their interviews and been accepted for service in Operation Self-Sacrifice. "I fully understand that this mission will end in my death."

It was a grim and solemn pledge for a young person to make.

But the young men who signed that pledge were full of patriotism and excited about the new planes they would be flying. Most of them were barely old enough to shave, only a year or two older than me. Sometimes I felt as if my sore heart was choking me as I watched these boys signing away their lives. What a waste of good pilots this mission was going to be! I knew I wasn't ever going to have to slam one of these planes into an enemy battleship myself, and it felt selfish that I was able to enjoy flying the Me-328. I hadn't agreed to give up my life for my country – why should anyone else?

But I wouldn't have dared to speak these thoughts aloud. In Hitler's Germany you disagreed in secret, in your head, or you got in trouble.

It had been the first crack in the fragile glass of my career in the Luftwaffe – learning that I was taking down names of young pilots who were going to pledge their lives to the Leonidas Squadron. But other cracks followed fast upon this first one.

I was waiting for Hanna to finish a test flight one morning, at an airfield near Stuttgart, when a plane came roaring in to land – a Messerschmitt-110 twin-engined fighter plane in full camouflage paint.

Two young men in Luftwaffe uniform climbed out. One of them called to the ground crew to ask directions to the operations building, but the other turned towards me. As I met his eyes, he gave me a wide and delighted smile.

"Ingrid!"

I gasped with surprise – these days, no one but Hanna ever called me by my first name. As this pilot pulled off his flying helmet, I recognised Emil Bruck.

He ran over and shook my hand warmly. "How lucky for us to land at the same airfield at the same time for once!" Emil said to me. "I was hoping I'd get to see the Flying Mouse do some of her signature corkscrews. Will you be in the air soon?"

I shook my head. "We are not p-p-performing here. Hanna's in the air on a t-t-t-test flight."

"Oh, too bad," Emil said. "I have to speak to the commander here, but after we've refuelled our plane we have to head straight back to our own base. How do you like being a flying circus star?"

I tried to smile – Emil was the one who got me this job, after all, and he must surely hope that I was doing well as the assistant to Flight Captain Hanna Reitsch. But I didn't think Emil knew about the Leonidas Squadron and Operation Self-Sacrifice. I wasn't going to be the one to risk his safety by sharing secrets he'd be better off not knowing, as Hanna had shared with me.

"I love flying the Hawk g-g-glider," I said, smiling. "But I do miss my real birds. I m-m-miss having animals about me."

Emil laughed and began to rummage in his flight bag.

"What are you d-d-d-doing here?" I asked. It was a relief to be able to talk to someone, other than Hanna, who didn't care about my stuttering.

"I'm delivering photographs we took last week," Emil explained. "Hold this, will you?" He handed me a cardboard folder and kept on searching in his bag, hunting for something else.

I opened the folder without thinking. The photograph on top showed a bird's eye view of a factory surrounded by rows of armoured tanks.

"No, don't look," Emil said sharply.

CHAPTER 17

I shut the folder quickly. I didn't want to get us into trouble. But the picture I'd seen stayed in my mind. Whose tanks were they? Ours, or the enemy's? What were they for? What battle would they fight?

"Hold on a moment," Emil said. "Here we are!"

He'd found what he was looking for in his bag and held it up triumphantly. It was a rare and wonderful prize only awarded to the military: a round tin of aviator chocolate.

"Have you ever tried this?" Emil asked me. "It's got coffee and kola mixed into it to give it a bit of zing to keep you awake on long flights. It's not a feast, but you know what Antoine de Saint-Exupéry says: 'We need to drink—'"

"'B-b-but also we need to communicate,'" I finished.

Emil grinned. "Swap you," he said, and held out the red and white tin of chocolate. I gave him back the folder. As he put the folder back into his bag, he said in a low voice, "You saw the tanks in that first photograph."

I nodded. It's true that I didn't want to risk trouble, but I couldn't help asking the question that burned in my mind: "Are they ours or ... or theirs?"

"Theirs," Emil answered. "Don't worry about it. We all know the Allied Nations are planning to attack us as soon as they build an army to invade, so they can force us to give up control over Europe. We're working on a plan to stop them. We think they'll start with Norway and northern France. I've had to make a lot of flights to England in the past month, trying to work out what equipment they've got."

I opened the tin and held it out to Emil, and he took out two shining wedges of dark chocolate. I had so many questions I wanted to ask him. How dangerous was it to take aerial photographs? Had a British fighter plane ever tried to shoot him down? Was his Messerschmitt-110 armed in case they did try?

What was the most interesting thing he'd ever had to photograph?

We wouldn't have more than a few minutes together. I didn't want to sound like an awestruck schoolgirl, peppering Emil with excited questions. So instead I said carefully, "I've had a chance to fly some n-n-new Luftwaffe planes. Thank you for recommending m-m-me ... I am so ... so lucky."

Emil didn't answer right away. He gave me one of the wedges of chocolate. I nibbled the tiniest bit off the point, and it was so sweet and bitter, so rich and wonderful, that it was almost painful to swallow.

"I've seen the factory where they make those new planes," said Emil. "I had to take some propaganda photos there. Ingrid ..."

He put his wedge of chocolate back into the tin I was still holding out.

"Ingrid, you should get out," Emil said. "Get out of the front line."

I didn't know what he meant. I wasn't a fighter pilot – I didn't have to fly combat missions, or risk being shot at by the enemy like Emil did. "I'm not ... not a coward!" I told him.

Emil shook his head. "I know you're not. I don't mean you should run away before the Allied Nations invade. I mean you should ..."

He hesitated just the way I did when I tried to prepare myself to speak without struggling.

At last Emil said, "Just ... stay away from the new planes. Keep as far away from them as you can. I've seen how poorly people are treated in the factories where those planes are built, and it makes me not want to go anywhere near them. They're poison. If you want to keep your conscience clean, walk away."

I didn't tell Emil that what he was saying made him sound like a traitor. I was sure he already knew that.

And I wanted to hear more. What was wrong with the way they built the new planes?

Emil didn't glance behind him to see if anyone was listening – it would have looked suspicious. He had to trust me to warn him if anyone came close.

"I've heard that the government is sending thousands of Jewish people and other non-Germanics to labour camps," Emil said, speaking softly. "You've heard that, haven't you, Ingrid?"

I nodded silently. I knew they took people away. We all knew that. They'd been taking people away for over ten years. But I also knew it was getting worse.

I lived in fear of it myself.

"Outside Germany they are saying terrible things about us," Emil went on. "Such as what we are doing to people who don't live up to the Führer's standards. One of the pilots in my squadron smuggled in a leaflet from Sweden. It said that in those labour camps, people are being put to death, killed in gas chambers – there are thousands and thousands of people being murdered every day."

Emil met my eyes, biting his lip.

I didn't want to believe him. But I remembered my mother coming home from work and weeping every day. I remembered those children who'd vanished from our village, and the letters telling the mayor and the butcher that their loved ones had died of pneumonia.

I shivered. I looked past Emil, scanning the airfield in case anyone came close enough to hear us talking. "Go on," I whispered.

"There were terrible photographs in the Swedish leaflet," Emil said. "Those who aren't killed are treated like ... like cattle. Worse than cattle. I don't know if I'd have believed it without seeing it, Ingrid. These slaves are starving. They're like stick figures. They get beaten if they don't do what they're told, and if they do what they're told they get poisoned and burnt by the materials in the factories ..."

That was what was waiting for me if I was sent there.

Emil took a deep breath and closed the lid on the rare and delicious aviator's chocolate.

"I'm sorry," he said. "I've upset you. We have such a short time to see each other, and I've ruined it."

I shook my head, shocked back into my normal silence.

"I can't get out," Emil said. "But you can. You can be a patriot and still have a conscience. *Get out now.*"

PART 4: *The Hawk*

CHAPTER 18

Of course I couldn't "get out" just because Emil told me to.

Spring was bursting around us. I woke every May morning just before dawn to a chorus of birdsong. My sore heart swelled, knowing that every one of these singers could take to the sky in freedom without having to think about the war.

We were in Stuttgart for a week, and every day Hanna and I were taken in a Luftwaffe staff car back and forth from our guesthouse to the airfield. On our last morning there, we were met at the airfield by a handsome, soft-spoken Luftwaffe legal officer. He didn't wait for Hanna to get out of the car as we pulled up in front of the operations building. Without a word, he handed Hanna a cardboard folder like Emil's through the open window of our car. Then the officer stood there with his hands linked behind his back, staring out over the airfield while Hanna read the loose pages that were tucked inside.

She collapsed like a balloon with the air let out.

In the time I'd known Hanna, she'd always been full of excitement and energy. But now she seemed like a child who'd put out her shoes by the window on St Nicholas Eve expecting treats and found them empty in the morning.

Hanna stared at the back of the driver's head. She didn't say anything. But she passed the pages to me to read.

It was an official letter telling Hanna that the Me-328s she'd ordered weren't going to be delivered. The factory where they'd been building them had been bombed, and the military instruction for them to be made had been destroyed in the bombing. Hanna's order for a thousand deadly aircraft had been cancelled.

No new order had been placed in another factory. The bombing had happened more than two weeks ago, and Hanna had only just found out about it.

I thought of those prisoners Emil had told me about, the people who were forced to build our new planes. He'd described these people as starving slaves, poisoned and burnt by the toxic materials they worked with. I wondered what had happened to them when the factory where they were forced to work was bombed.

I glanced up from the page to look at Flight Captain Hanna Reitsch, still staring quietly ahead. She must be thinking exactly what I was thinking: she might be a celebrity, but she had no real authority in the Luftwaffe.

Without aircraft, there could be no Leonidas Squadron.

Hanna's hands were tensed into clenched fists against her thighs. She wasn't just disappointed, she was angry too.

I didn't say anything to try to comfort her. The legal officer would hear whatever I said.

Also, I may have felt sorry for Hanna, but deep in my heart I felt a treacherous spark of hope and relief. I didn't *want* eager recruits plunging to their deaths to destroy a few Allied battleships. It made me sick that the aircraft I loved so well were created by prisoners working as slaves. These miserable people were being forced to make bombs that would destroy any hope of rescue for them. And I knew that if he heard me trying to speak, the man standing outside the car might send me to a similar fate.

After another minute or so, Hanna opened the car door. The legal officer was still standing there. His face was blank – he didn't look as if he cared or even knew what news he'd just delivered to Hanna. But he must have taken a look at that letter before he gave it to her – it hadn't been sealed.

"I expect you won't be flying today, Flight Captain Reitsch," the officer said to her. He took hold of the car door to open it wide so Hanna could climb out.

I climbed out behind her and she turned to look at me. "We'll have to go back to the original plan and use the Doodlebugs," she said. She nodded to herself, thinking about it, but she sounded tired and angry as she spoke. "Unlike the Me-328, the Doodlebug wasn't designed to carry a pilot ..."

I knew that no one was trained to fly Doodlebugs. Several experienced test pilots had already been killed trying to fly them, and Germany was running out of time. The Allied nations were planning to invade Europe – they were putting together an army to try to take power away from the Führer and the Third Reich. We had to have a plan in place before the attack came.

I watched the Luftwaffe legal officer hold back a laugh, and I hated him.

Hanna stood up to him, not in the least bit daunted, despite being so small a woman that the top of her head only came up to his shoulder.

"We'd have been prepared for this setback if we had designed a training programme for the Doodlebugs last year, *as I suggested*," she said angrily. "Now we'll have to start from scratch. And meanwhile …"

Hanna didn't finish her sentence. But I guessed that she was thinking the same thing I was again – the Allied invasion would begin any day now. Maybe she hadn't seen the pictures that I'd seen, but I was sure she knew that there were enemy tanks lined up and ready to be shipped to France and Norway. They'd bring American and British and Canadian soldiers with them, and Germany would have to fight a ground war in Western Europe as well as the one that was already raging on the Eastern Front in Russia. The Luftwaffe was running short of fuel and planes and experienced pilots, and we didn't have time for a new training programme.

I'd noticed the first crack in the fragile glass of my Luftwaffe career almost as soon as I'd joined Hanna, on the day that I'd reluctantly collected names of young volunteers for the Leonidas Squadron. Now that glass was covered in damage, impossible to see through, ready to shatter – like the cockpit canopy of a fighter plane that has been hit with enemy fire.

Emil had told me to get out. But like a pilot in a damaged plane, I had to keep flying blindly before I was able to land.

CHAPTER 19

The Allied invasion stunned everybody. Their forces didn't strike at Norway or the part of France closest to Great Britain as we'd expected. Those tanks that Emil had photographed were dummies, meant to fool us. On 6 June 1944, the Allies attacked in Normandy, more difficult for them to get to, but easier to take us by surprise. It was the largest seaborne invasion in history.

Our soldiers on the ground and our Luftwaffe fighters and bombers fought hard against the Allied Nations' enormous army. Anyone who wasn't fighting was put to work supporting those who were.

Two weeks after the invasion began, our government launched the Doodlebugs as unmanned flying bombs. They hurled them against Great Britain in a storm of retaliation and fear. They would never be used as suicide aircraft now. They weren't able to aim the Doodlebugs at an accurate target, but over the wide stretches of the city of

London they did damage wherever they fell – and they terrified people.

I thought of Emil and what he'd said about the factories where those bombs were made. The factory where they'd made the Me-328 aircraft had been destroyed, but plenty of other factories were still producing aircraft and weapons as fast as they could turn them out. Were people dying while making the flying bombs, as well as those who died when they reached their target?

I knew that Hanna justified her war work by trying to save lives with as few deaths as possible. I tried to comfort her by pointing out that if she couldn't use the Doodlebugs, she wouldn't have those factory workers on her conscience.

"What on earth are you talking about, Ingrid?" Hanna asked.

"We are ... are using slaves to make our bombs and p-p-planes," I told her.

"That is a lie!" Hanna protested wearily. "I've heard those rumours. There's no proof whatsoever. It's propaganda spread by our enemies."

I knew Hanna well by now – I knew she didn't like to hear uncomfortable truths. And I also knew that she was so focused on her own plans that she could be utterly blind to what was going on around her.

I had no evidence myself of what happened to those factory workers. But Emil wasn't just a pilot – he was also a photographer. His job was to record things carefully and make conclusions based on what he saw. I didn't think he would lie to me about what he'd *seen*.

"It's n-n-not just ..." I hesitated, not because I was stuttering, or because I knew I'd struggle with the word "propaganda", but because I was suddenly worried that Emil would get in trouble if I told Hanna where I'd heard the rumours.

So I shut up.

"N-n-never mind," I said.

But it probably wouldn't have mattered whether I'd mentioned Emil or not.

He was already in trouble.

CHAPTER 20

I wondered if this was the end of my war work – if I wasn't able to do anything useful any more for Hanna or for the air force. What would happen to me when Hanna stopped giving air displays for new pilots? I knew so much more than I should about the air force's secrets. Would I be sent to a labour camp to keep me quiet?

The thought made me feel sick.

Almost, *almost*, I wished that Hanna would send me home to Ulmenhain.

Almost. I knew that going home wouldn't really make me any safer or restore my faith in my nation.

But Hanna had other flight tests to work on, and still she kept me at her side. She thought our display flights were good for morale. She'd visited our soldiers on the Eastern Front in Russia eight months ago to cheer them up, and now she wanted to do the same for our soldiers on the Second Front in France. We'd stay there for three weeks, just as she'd done in Russia last autumn.

So our Hawk gliders got packed up and delivered across Germany and then France in a lorry. Meanwhile Hanna and I managed to get a ride in a transport plane to meet the lorry driver at an airfield which the Allied forces hadn't reached yet. Here, we'd perform together to raise the spirits of the Luftwaffe Air Groups as they stopped to refuel on their way to the Second Front, where the fighting against the Allied forces continued.

I'd never been so close to the real battles of war before. There weren't any passenger seats in the Junkers transport aircraft we were flying in, so Hanna and I crouched behind the pilot and navigator so that we could look out of the windscreen of the front cockpit. We could see black puffs of anti-aircraft bullets peppering the sky ahead of us. The flying here would be more dangerous than anything I'd ever done.

The big transport plane landed smoothly. I stuck to Hanna like glue as we waited for our display gliders to arrive. The airmen and ground crew at this makeshift French airfield were grim and silent, but a few of them stared with hungry eyes at us two young women. War had hardened them.

Then, to my astonishment and joy, I recognised Emil again when he leapt from the cockpit of a Messerschmitt Me-110 along with his navigator – the very morning that our gliders arrived in the transport lorry.

Hanna was supervising the ground crew who were unloading the Hawk gliders from the lorry, but I welcomed Emil with a smile of relief and delight.

He swaggered over to me and embraced me as if we were lovers. He kissed me hard, with his hands under the tunic of my uniform, pulling at the back of my skirt.

I struggled against Emil, shocked. He was dear to me, an old friend from home, but we'd never been lovers – in fact I'd never kissed *anyone* before. And we were standing in full view of a dozen staring soldiers, not to mention Flight Captain Hanna Reitsch herself!

Emil took a step backward. I glared at him with my mouth open, and he raised one finger briefly to his lips as if he were telling me to hush.

I felt betrayed.

"You—" I gasped. But as he dropped his other hand from my waist, I realised that he'd tucked something into the waistband at the back of my skirt, pulling my tunic down over the top to hide it.

"No enemy left in all the world," said Emil softly. He leaned close to my ear and whispered quickly, "Get out, Ingrid. You're close enough to the front now that you *really can get out*. I can't – my navigator would shoot me if I tried. But you're always on your own in your Hawk. Next time you're in the sky, take your conscience and mine and cross the line. Tell the Allies what our government is doing to us – what it's doing to people all over Europe. All right? Now hit me across the face as if you hate me. I think I'm about to be arrested. I don't want to get you in trouble along with me."

Still I stared at him, not daring to move or speak in case I did something wrong.

"*Hit me hard*," Emil said, waiting for it.

So I did.

I struck him across the face so hard that he staggered.

"How d-d-dare you!" I cried. My voice rang shrill in my ears, and I bit my lip, worrying that my outburst would attract attention to my stutter.

I turned my back on my friend and stormed away. The package he had tucked into my waistband made me feel like my back was on fire.

But Emil had risked his life to put it there, so now I was going to have to risk mine to keep it secret until I found out what it was.

CHAPTER 21

Emil had given me proof.

He'd given me an envelope full of photographs.

I looked at them by the light of an electric torch under my blanket that night. He'd somehow taken these pictures of the workers at the flying-bomb factory site – skinny slaves in striped prison suits, their heads shaved bald, pulling carts like mules. A pile of skeletal naked bodies beside an incinerator oven. A flinching man being beaten with a chain by a uniformed officer. And there were more, all unspeakable and unimaginable.

My first thought was to run and wave these at Hanna. *See? See? Proof! Be thankful you're no longer working on Operation Self-Sacrifice!*

But then I saw the other photographs Emil had given me: overhead views of factories and airfields. Pictures of our newest aircraft rolling off a production line. A launch site for the flying bombs.

Tell the Allies what our government is doing to us, Emil had said.

He'd handed me these photographs in secret and told me to *get out*. He'd told me to take my plane over the front and *cross the line*.

He didn't want me to show these pictures to Hanna. There wasn't anything she'd be able to do with them.

He wanted me to show them to the Allies.

I knew what I had to do with these photographs. I just didn't know if I had the bravery to do it.

*

I kept the photographs in my waistband because I didn't dare to leave them anywhere they might be found.

I soared and rolled in the sky to raise the spirits of the young soldiers who were going to fly into battle a few hours later. But I was so distracted that I nearly clipped Hanna's wing as we turned over each other in the air in our Hawks.

Hanna landed ahead of me, as always. I circled above her, riding the wind and waiting for the right moment to land. I stared out at the smoky horizon and at the murky puffs of explosions that marked the line of the battle front.

If I climbed high enough, I could just about glide down to land on the other side of that line.

But I didn't.

I landed behind Hanna the way I was supposed to.

I wasn't quite bold enough to cross the front.

CHAPTER 22

Three days later, we arrived at the next airfield for another propaganda performance, and there was a parcel waiting for me. It had been chasing me across Germany, posted two months ago. Every time it arrived at an airfield where I'd been, I'd already moved on. Our visit to the Second Front in France was the first time I'd stayed long enough for the parcel to catch up with me. It was wrapped in brown paper that was criss-crossed with forwarding addresses.

The parcel was from my father in Ulmenhain.

I opened it with trembling hands. Inside the brown paper was the book I'd borrowed from Emil: *Wind, Sand and Stars* by the French pilot Antoine de Saint-Exupéry.

My father had tucked a note in it.

My dear Ingrid,

I know this was your favourite book of the past year, as I have seen you so often absorbed in it. I confess that I have often wondered why you should be so obsessed with a popular novel written by a Frenchman. But then I listened to the chatter of your birds at the feeding table in our garden and I thought of you in the sky, and so I read this work before I sent it on. And now I believe I understand why you have always been so happy in the air. Saint-Exupéry brings to life the joy of flying, which you are lucky enough to be able to experience also.

Flight Captain Reitsch has written to tell me that you are obedient, willing and capable as her assistant. I hope you are happy in the air wherever this finds you, and that your war work is fulfilling. I am glad that you are able to combine serving the country with your passion for flying. As Saint-Exupéry says, we need to drink, but we also need to communicate.

*Your mother and I both knew how hard
you have always struggled to communicate.
She would have been proud of you, using
your skills in the service of your country.
I hope that your heart is not broken by that
service, as hers was. I am proud of you too.
You have the power of flight, and maybe
that will give you new chances to share
your knowledge.*

*Remember your father, who in his own
way also struggles to communicate.*

Two phrases in this letter struck me deeply:
Remember your father. And also: *You have the
power of flight, and maybe that will give you new
chances to share your knowledge.*

My father could not possibly have known
the dilemma I would be facing when I received
his letter. He could not know that I had been
given a secret mission to share information with
Germany's enemies that might help them to win
the war. He could not know that the power of flight
would give me the ability to complete that mission,
if I had the bravery to do it.

My father gave me the bravery I needed.

The next time I took to the sky in my Hawk, I knew I would not come back.

I took Emil's photographs with me – the damning photographs that told how Germany was enslaving prisoners, and where our factories were, and what our new planes were like. I kept them tucked into the back of my waistband where Emil had put them when he first gave them to me. I remembered his kiss, and wished it had not been a pretence, or that it had been gentler, or that it had happened somewhere else and for a different reason.

I wondered if Emil had been arrested as he had feared – and if his fate had been the same one I so dreaded for myself. I wondered if he was already dead.

This was for Emil then, alive or dead. For my mother's memory – and for my father, alive and clinging to hope. This was for a brighter future for Germany. I was determined I would follow the flight of the hawks between updrafts. I would have to fly the longest distance I'd ever flown, without power. I would risk being shot down by the

Allies' guns when they saw my enemy aircraft. If I survived, I would become a prisoner of war.

Would I ever come back to Germany? I realised that I had no idea what my future would hold, how far this journey would take me, or for how long.

Perhaps, in that unknown future, I would learn to speak a new language. Perhaps, starting afresh, I might at last be able to speak my thoughts aloud without stuttering. I needed to communicate as much as I needed to drink, or to eat, or to breathe.

But even if I did stutter, I would have no enemy left in all the world.

Heave! Double strength! Away!

I heard the words in my head as the rope released my Hawk glider.

I was in the sky, alone. I could see the smoke of battle rising at the Second Front, where the other side waited for me.

I soared to cross the line.

AUTHOR'S NOTE

One of the great challenges of writing historical fiction is how to tell a story about a real person that stays true to the facts while adding imaginary characters and plot. In *The Last Hawk*, I made up the character of Ingrid Hartman and her role in the Luftwaffe. But the test pilot Hanna Reitsch and her ideas for winning the war and the aircraft she flew were all real.

The Nazi Party discouraged German women from getting a higher education, wanting them to be mothers and caregivers. But throughout the 1930s the Nazis embraced the idea of using women pilots as ambassadors of the skies. They hoped to cover up their deadly plans for aviation by showcasing the flight skills and achievements of a few people with pretty faces and charm.

When I started writing, I knew I wanted Ingrid to be a pilot, but it occurred to me she would be a more complex character if she was struggling with personal issues that had nothing to do with flying. What I did not realise was that by giving her a stutter I was also putting her life in danger. I discovered more about the Nazi Party's policies on disabilities and genetic disorders, and I realised that Ingrid's stutter was going to be a plot point as well as part of what shaped her personality.

Stuttering – or stammering – is a communication disorder in which a person's speech is disrupted. The speaker repeats sounds or syllables, makes them longer, or gets stuck trying to say a word. It is over three times more common in boys than in girls. Stuttering normally begins to show at an early age as a person learns to speak. What causes it isn't entirely understood, but developmental stuttering may be inherited. Stuttering can also be caused in later life by brain trauma such as a stroke or a head injury.

Many children who stutter stop as they grow older. It is not a mental disorder, nor is it an indicator of intelligence. It is not a sign of nervousness or shyness or lack of confidence – however, the frustration and stress it causes may affect the speaker's confidence. People who stutter can be confident speakers. Ingrid is not a confident speaker, but that is because her experience has been shaped by a real fear for her life as she grows up under Nazi rule. I liked the idea of balancing her lack of confidence in speaking with her solid skill and ability as a pilot.

If you are interested in learning more about stuttering, or are affected by it yourself, you can find support online, such as the British Stammering Association at stamma.org and the American National Stuttering Association at westutter.org.

While I invented Ingrid's role as Hanna Reitsch's assistant, it is true that there were women pilots serving their country in Germany in the Second World War. By the end of the war, at least five German women were working as ferry pilots for the Luftwaffe. In 1944, about sixty German women were recruited by the National Socialist Flyer Corps to become gliding instructors, and a few others served Germany as test pilots for new aircraft. All these women were colourful characters, but Hanna Reitsch's wartime experience is by far the most dramatic.

She really did perform flight tests in the Doodlebug flying bomb, and she really did champion Operation Self-Sacrifice and the Leonidas Squadron. She was the only test pilot who could safely control the Doodlebug in flight, and she really did complain that it glided about as well as a piano!

Hanna's other amazing accomplishments include being the first woman to fly a helicopter (she gave several demonstrations to an audience *inside a sports hall*), flying a rocket in a test flight, and landing a Stork reconnaissance plane in the middle of a Berlin park to deliver the new head of the Luftwaffe to a meeting with Hitler. I have tried to recreate Hanna's remarkable personality as she describes herself in her autobiography, *The Sky My Kingdom*, and as others saw her: an incredibly talented woman who adored flying, who often acted ignorantly in her desire to be patriotic, and who could be unbelievably blind to what was going on around her.

All the amazing aircraft mentioned in *The Last Hawk* are real, along with the terrifying plans for launching them and using them in war – real schemes proposed and tested by the German aircraft designers and military experts in the Second World War. There weren't many military officials who shared Hanna's passion for Operation Self-Sacrifice, but she did get about seventy volunteers to sign her suicide pledge. After the Allies invaded Normandy, the plan of Operation Self-Sacrifice was abandoned because of lack of materials and support, and because it was impractical to waste good pilots.

I simplified the creation of the Leonidas Squadron in this book, but I believe that its essence is represented faithfully. I tweaked the timeline and Hanna's movements during the summer of 1944 to keep the fictional story tight. The damning Swedish leaflet and photographs that Emil describes to Ingrid were inspired by something that happened to Hanna in October 1944, when a fellow pilot tried to convince her of the horrors that took place in the concentration camps. Hanna simply refused to believe that her beloved nation could be supporting something so terrible.

Speaking of photographs, there is an interesting story behind the "tanks" that Ingrid sees among the pictures Emil tells her he took flying over England. These dummy tanks were inflatable or made of wood and were part of a complex Allied plan called "Operation Fortitude". This was designed to mislead German intelligence about where the Allied invasion of Europe would take place. The true landing site, in Normandy, was such an important secret that on the night of the invasion, Allied planes dropped dummy parachutists elsewhere to distract the German forces from the real Allied paratroopers.

One of my tricks for pulling together a story and making it feel real and personal is to include details from everyday life. The aviator chocolate that Emil shares with Ingrid was a German invention of the 1930s, called "Scho-Ka-Kola". During the war it was given to pilots and soldiers to give them a boost of energy during long sleepless missions. It's still available today and still packaged in a distinctive red and white tin. I tried some myself while I was writing *The Last Hawk*!

I like to include things in my books that I've tested or experienced, and the French aviation writer Antoine de Saint-Exupéry is the author of some of my own favourite books. He's best known for his global bestseller *The Little Prince*. I liked the idea of Ingrid being a keen reader and did some background research to find out if Saint-Exupéry's famous autobiographical book, *Wind, Sand and Stars*, was published in Germany in the 1930s.

I was delighted to discover that German pilots of the time adored this book, and I was able to use that as a theme in *The Last Hawk*. I based Emil's passion for it on an account from the German pilot Horst Rippert, who it's believed shot down and killed Saint-Exupéry on 31 July 1944. Rippert was sick at heart when he discovered he'd been responsible for the death of the famous writer and called it a catastrophe. He said he would never have fired a shot if he'd known who was in the other plane.

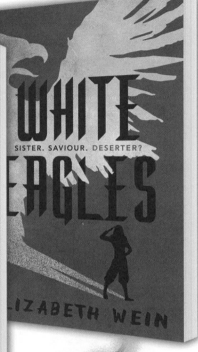

978-1-78112-831-2

978-1-78112-896-1

MORE FROM
ELIZABETH WEIN

Our books are tested
for children and young people by
children and young people.

Thanks to everyone who consulted on
a manuscript for their time and effort in
helping us to make our books better
for our readers.